Disney
fairies

Tink
in a
Fairy
Fix

Tink
in a
Fairy
Fix

WRITTEN BY
KIKI THORPE

ILLUSTRATED BY
DENISE SHIMABUKURO,
DEE FARNSWORTH & LOREN CONTRERAS

RANDOM HOUSE 🏠 NEW YORK

Library of Congress Cataloging-in-Publication Data

Thorpe, Kiki.

Tink in a fairy fix / written by Kiki Thorpe ; illustrated by Denise
Shimabukuro, Dee Farnsworth & Loren Contreras.

p.   cm.

Summary: When Tinkerbell runs low on pots and pans to repair, she
begins trying to fix fairies instead, whether they want her help or not.

ISBN 978-0-7364-2661-9 (pbk.)

*[1. Problem solving—Fiction. 2. Fairies—Fiction.] I. Shimabukuro, Denise,
ill. II. Farnsworth, Dee, ill. III. Contreras, Loren, ill. IV. Title.*

PZ7.T3974Tiq 2011

[E]—dc22   2010046459

www.randomhouse.com/kids

Printed in the United States of America

10 9 8 7 6 5 4 3 2 1

All About Fairies

IF YOU HEAD toward the second star on your right and fly straight on till morning, you'll come to Never Land, a magical island where mermaids play and children never grow up.

When you arrive, you might hear something like the tinkling of little bells. Follow that sound and you'll find Pixie Hollow, the secret heart of Never Land.

A great old maple tree grows in Pixie

Hollow, and in it live hundreds of fairies and sparrow men. Some of them can do water magic, others can fly like the wind, and still others can speak to animals. You see, Pixie Hollow is the Never fairies' kingdom, and each fairy who lives there has a special, extraordinary talent.

Not far from the Home Tree, nestled in the branches of a hawthorn, is Mother Dove, the most magical creature of all. She sits on her egg, watching over the fairies, who in turn watch over her. For as long as Mother Dove's egg stays well and whole, no one in Never Land will ever grow old.

Once, Mother Dove's egg *was* broken. But we are not telling the story of the egg here. Now it is time for Tink's tale. . . .

Disney
fairies

Tink
in a
Fairy
Fix

1

"PERFECT!" Tinker Bell declared.

She set aside her tinker's hammer and held up the watering can she'd been fixing. She turned it this way and that, admiring her work.

The watering can was made of tin and had a long, curving spout. It belonged to Tink's friend Lily, a garden-talent fairy.

When Lily had brought it to Tink, it had a big hole in the bottom and was full of dents and dings. Tink had fixed the hole and hammered out all the dents. She'd even added a fresh coat of gloss. Now there wasn't a single scratch. For Tink, nothing was ever finished until it was good as new.

It was this sort of fine tinkering that made Tink the best pots-and-pans fairy in Pixie Hollow.

"One of my better jobs, if I do say so myself," Tink said. She put down the can. Then she turned to the workbench where she kept all the broken pots and cracked pans and other things waiting to be fixed.

To her surprise, the bench was empty.

She glanced around her workshop, hoping to spy a twisted ladle or a forgotten serving fork—anything that needed fixing. But there was nothing. Not a single teaspoon.

A disappointed sigh escaped Tink's lips. What was she going to do now? Fixing things wasn't only Tink's job, it was her favorite pastime. She liked it better than just about anything.

"Well, I guess I'll take this watering can back to Lily," she said at last. Picking up the can, she flew out the door.

Outside, Pixie Hollow was buzzing with activity. Garden fairies flittered among the flowers. Message-talent fairies darted by, delivering the daily news. Animal-talent fairies watched over the dairy mice. Tink spotted her friend Rani, a water-talent fairy, sailing a leaf-boat down Havendish Stream. Tink waved, and Rani waved back.

Humming to herself, Tink spread her wings and set out for Lily's garden. But she hadn't gotten far when she heard a loud *SCREEEEECH!*

Startled, Tink pulled up short. She heard the sound again. *SCREEEECH! SCREEEEECH!*

The hairs on Tink's neck stood on end. What in the name of Never Land was making that horrible noise?

Tink looked right. She looked left. She looked down . . . and spotted a mouse-drawn cart making its way slowly over the mossy ground. One of the wheels went SCREEEEEEEEEEECCCH! SCREEEEEEEEEEECCCH!

The driver, a sparrow man named Dooley, didn't seem to notice. He was singing loudly. His sad song floated up to Tink's ears.

> *"I've got a squeaky wheel*
> *And an ear full of fluff.*
> *My nose is itchin'.*
> *As if that weren't enough,*
> *My cart is heavy.*
> *The mice are unruly.*
> *It's a sad, sad day*
> *For poor old Dooley."*

Every few words, the wheel chimed in with a SCREEEECH!

"Why doesn't Dooley do something about that wheel?" Tink wondered out loud. "That sound is awful! It's . . . it's . . ."

Tink's heart suddenly gave a little leap. It was the sound of something that needed to be fixed!

She quickly landed in the road. Dooley stopped the cart and looked down at her. He had a long, droopy face and big, sad eyes. "Fly with you, Tinker Bell," he said in greeting. "Is something the matter?"

"You have a squeaky wheel," Tink said. "It's making an awful racket!"

Dooley cupped a hand to his pointed ear. "What's that?"

"I *said*"—Tink raised her voice—"you have a squeaky wheel!"

"Sorry, Tink, I can't hear you," Dooley said. He reached into his ears and pulled

out two big wads of dandelion fluff. At once, he let out an enormous sneeze. "*AHH-CHOO!*"

The mice jumped, jerking the cart around.

"Whoa!" Dooley tugged on the reins. "The mice don't like it when I sneeze," he explained to Tink. "But I can't help it. The dandelion fluff makes my nose itch."

"Then why do you put it in your ears?" she asked.

"Because I have a squeaky wheel," Dooley replied. "It's making an awful racket. I'm surprised you didn't hear it, Tink." He pulled a leafkerchief out of his pocket and blew his nose. "That's better. Now, what were you saying?"

Tink rolled her eyes. "Hold your mice for a minute, and I'll see if I can fix your wheel." She put down the watering can and darted around to the side of the cart.

"Dooley, this wheel is covered with rust! No wonder it's squeaking!" Tink exclaimed.

"Yes," Dooley said sadly. "Got caught in the rain, I did. As if that weren't bad enough, now I've got a squeaky wheel. Poor, poor me." He shook his head. "There's nothing to be done about it, though."

"Of course something can be done about it," Tink said. "It just needs some oil. Wait right here."

Tink flew into her workshop. She was back moments later with an oilcan.

Dooley climbed down from the cart. He stood beside Tink, watching as she oiled the wheel. "I don't suppose it will work," he said gloomily.

Tink gave the wheel an experimental spin. *SCREEEECH*.

"I knew it couldn't be fixed," Dooley said as Tink added oil. "Nothing ever

goes right for me. Today it's a squeaky wheel. Tomorrow it will be a leaky roof or a lump in my porridge. It's a squeaky, leaky, lumpy life for poor old—"

"There!" Tink set down the oilcan and spun the wheel. It whirled smoothly. "I fixed it!"

Dooley blinked. "Well, I'll be. So you did."

Tink oiled the rest of the wheels. Then she tucked the oilcan into the back of Dooley's cart. "Keep this," she told him. "You can oil the wheels whenever they squeak."

"That's very kind of you, Tink," said Dooley. "Now I'd best be on my way."

Dooley climbed into the driver's seat. He tucked the dandelion fluff back into his ears and sneezed twice. *"AHH-CHOO! AHH-CHOO!"*

The mice leaped forward, startled.

"Whoa!" cried Dooley, tugging on the reins. He shook his head sadly. "Itchy nose. Unhappy mice. Nothing ever goes right for me. Ah, well. That's just the way it is." He clucked at the mice, and the cart started down the road.

"Dooley, wait!" Tink called after him.

Dooley stopped the cart. He squinted down at Tink. "Now what is it?"

"I fixed your wheel. It doesn't squeak anymore," Tink reminded him.

Dooley nodded patiently. "That's right, you did. Very kind of you, Tink."

"But don't you see? If your wheel doesn't squeak, you don't need to put dandelion fluff in your ears," Tink told him.

"Hmmm. I suppose I don't," Dooley said. He took the fluff out.

"And if you don't have fluff in your ears, your nose won't itch," Tink continued. "And if your nose doesn't itch, you won't sneeze. And if you don't sneeze, you won't scare the mice."

Dooley's eyes got rounder. He touched his nose. Then he turned toward the mice. They stood calmly in their harnesses, chewing bits of hayseed.

"Well, I'll be!" Dooley exclaimed. And suddenly, he smiled. It was a big, beautiful, beaming smile. Tink realized she'd never seen him smile before.

"It seems things are going my way after

all!" Dooley doffed his cap to Tink. Then he set off down the road again, singing.

> "My wheel is rolling.
> I'm on my way.
> The mice are happy
> With their bit of hay.
> The sun is shining.
> I think it's truly
> A lucky day
> For good old Dooley!"

"Funny old Dooley." Tink chuckled to herself. Then, picking up Lily's watering can, she went on her way.

2

"LILY!" TINK CALLED. She peered into the heart of Lily's garden. Poppies, bluebells, and buttercups grew together in a colorful jumble.

Tink brushed past a cluster of lilac blossoms. "Lily!" she called again. "Are you here?" There was no answer. Tink landed on the petal of a large golden flower and looked around the garden.

"Don't step on the daylilies!" some-one squawked. The voice was loud and shrill.

Tink spun around. She came face to face with a curly-haired fairy sitting on a leaf. The fairy, whose name was Iris, scowled. "Didn't you hear me? No dilly-dallying on the daylilies!"

Tink quickly hopped off the flower. "I was just looking for Lily."

"That doesn't mean you can go around using her daylilies as a doormat," snapped Iris.

That voice! It sent a shudder down Tink's spine. It was every bit as screechy as Dooley's squeaky wheel.

Iris studied the petal where Tink had

been standing, as if inspecting it for foot-prints. "*Tsk-tsk.*" She darted over to a fat book that lay open on a leaf and jotted something down.

"What are you writing?" Tink asked worriedly. The petal had looked all right to her.

Iris glanced up. "It's garden-fairy business," she huffed. "None of your concern." She went back to writing.

Like Lily, Iris was a garden-talent fairy. She kept a big book about all the plants in Pixie Hollow, and she was always writing in it.

There was still no sign of Lily. Tink decided to find a place to sit and wait for her. But each time she tried to land, Iris stopped her.

"Mind the marigolds!" Iris called. "Don't sit near those daisies—they just bloomed! And don't you dare disturb the baby's breath. It needs its rest!"

Tink hovered in midair and sighed loudly. She hoped Lily would show up soon.

"Tinker Bell," a gentle voice behind her said.

Tink turned. "Lily! There you are!"

Lily set down the basket of seeds she was carrying and hugged Tink. "It's nice of you to drop by."

"I brought your watering can," Tink told her.

"And she trod on the tallest daylily," Iris tattled from her leaf.

Tink hung her head. "I didn't mean to—"

But Lily just waved her hand. "Don't worry, Tink. Daylilies can be hardy. They can stand up to a few fairy footprints. Now, I can't wait to see my old watering can. I know I have others. But this was the first one I got when I Arrived."

"Good as new." Tink held it up proudly.

Lily took the can. As she looked at it, her smile dimmed a little.

"Is something wrong?" Tink asked.

"Well . . . ," Lily said. "It's just that it's so *perfect.* . . ."

"Exactly," Tink agreed happily.

"But it doesn't really look like *my* watering can," Lily finished.

"Oh, it is!" Tink assured her. "I just fixed the hole and hammered out all the dents and dings and gave it a fresh coat of paint. Don't you like it?"

Lily nodded. "It's very nice. But," she added more quietly, "I'll miss some of those dents and dings. They were sort of like old friends."

Iris had been pretending to be busy with her book. But now her curiosity got the better of her. She flew over to see the watering can.

"I don't see what all the fuss is about an old tin can," she sniffed. "Why, any gardening fairy knows the *best* watering cans are made of copper."

Tink rolled her eyes. Why did Iris have to be so *rude?*

But Lily hardly seemed to notice Iris's behavior. She turned back to Tink. "I wonder if you would take a look at my gardening rake. There's something wrong with it."

Lily led Tink over to a small toolshed. The rake was leaning up against the wall.

"Oh!" Tink gasped. The rake hardly looked like a rake at all. Its tines were twisted together like a snarl of spaghetti. Its handle was nearly broken in half. "What happened?"

"I had a tangle with some tangleroot," Lily replied. "And the root won. It's my only rake, so I hate to throw it away. But a rake that doesn't rake isn't much use, is it?"

Tink agreed that it was not. "I might be able to fix it," she said.

"Could you?" asked Lily hopefully.

Tink grinned. Fixing the rake would be challenging—and she loved a challenge! "Leave it to me," she told Lily. Taking the rake by the handle, she turned to go.

"Don't hit the hollyhocks on the way out!" Iris called after her.

What an unpleasant fairy, thought Tink. Shaking her head, she flew away.

Tink was eager to start fixing the rake. But when she got to her workshop, Spring, a message-talent fairy, was standing on the doorstep.

"There you are, Tink!" Spring exclaimed. "I've been looking all over for you. Tell me—what did you do to Dooley?"

"What do you mean?" Tink asked in surprise. "What's the matter with him?"

"Not a thing!" Spring informed her cheerfully. "That's just it. He's glad as can be. Going around with a happy song on his lips and a smile for every fairy he meets."

"*Dooley?*" Tink asked in astonishment.

Spring nodded. "He's completely changed. And he says it's all thanks to you, Tink."

"*Me?*"

"So how did you do it? Everyone wants to know." Spring raised her eyebrows.

"But . . . all I did was fix a wheel on his cart," Tink said.

"I'd say you fixed more than that," said Spring. When Tink didn't reply, she added, "Is it a tinker-fairy secret? Don't worry, you can tell me." Spring leaned toward Tink, her eyes twinkling. Message-talent fairies loved secrets.

"I don't know," Tink said with a shrug. "I just oiled the wheel on his cart. I'd better get to work now, Spring. I've got Lily's garden rake to fix."

"If you ask me, you're wasting your time with pots and pans and garden rakes," Spring replied. "You could be using your talent for bigger things." She waved and darted off.

Tink stared after her. "Bigger things?" she echoed. "*What* bigger things?"

But Spring had already flown away.

3

"Now, HOW SHOULD I fix this rake?" Tink asked herself as she went into her workshop. Just as she picked up her tinker's hammer, the bell over her door jingled. A fairy poked her head inside.

"What is it?" Tink said with a scowl. She didn't like to be bothered while she was working.

But when she looked up, Tink forgot to be annoyed. The fairy standing in the doorway was an astonishing sight. She wore a dandelion-leaf tunic over a poppy-petal dress topped by a pink-carnation tutu. Her cornsilk stockings were tucked into purple pansy slippers with twice-curled toes. And on top of her head, she wore *three* hats—a purple puff, a daisy sunshade, and a pink raspberry beret. A small, round face poked out from all that finery. This was Trindle, a sewing-talent fairy.

"Fly with you, Trindle," said Tink, trying to hide her surprise. "What can I do for you?"

Trindle hovered just inside the doorway. She looked around uncertainly.

"I need your help," she told Tink.

"With what?" Tink asked, getting excited. "A leaky pot? Or a dented pan? Or . . ." She trailed off, noticing that Trindle's hands were empty.

"I can't decide," Trindle whispered.

"You can't decide if it's a pot or a pan?" asked Tink, confused.

"I can't decide anything!" Trindle exclaimed. "I can't decide if I should wear a blue cloak or a yellow jacket. I can't decide if I should wear a red skirt or green overalls. I simply cannot decide!"

"Oh," Tink said. Why was Trindle telling her this?

"So, do you think you can help me?" Trindle asked. "They say you're the best fix-it fairy around."

"Oh!" Suddenly Tink understood. Trindle wanted Tink to fix *her*! "But I don't fix fairies," Tink explained. "I only fix pots and pans."

"Please, Tink!" Trindle begged. "I don't know what else to do!" One of Trindle's hats slipped down over her eyes. She pushed it back and looked pleadingly at Tink.

"Like I was saying, I don't—" Tink broke off. Beneath all those hats, Trindle looked so small and sad. Tink couldn't help feeling sorry for her.

Maybe there is something I can do, Tink thought. After all, she was good at fixing pots and pans. How different could fixing a fairy be?

"Tell me more," she said.

Trindle sat down in a chair next to Tink. "It's the same every morning," she explained. "I open the doors to my closet and ask myself, 'What should I wear today?'"

"I don't see how it matters," said Tink, who wore more or less the same thing every day.

Trindle gasped. "Oh, but it does! The clothes you wear say so much about you! But I'm never sure what I want to say. Should I wear yellow sunflower petals to say I'm feeling sunny? Or should I say I'm feeling pretty in pink primroses? Or that I'm feeling bright in red begonias? In the end, I can't decide. So I pile everything on at once."

"It sounds complicated," said Tink.

"It is," Trindle agreed. "Not to mention hot."

Tink looked at Trindle thoughtfully. In her colorful clothes, Trindle reminded Tink of a fancy cake. Of course, thinking of cakes made Tink think of cake pans. And thinking about cake pans made her think of ovens. And from there it wasn't long before her thoughts turned to oven timers, which often needed fixing.

"Tink?" asked Trindle, waving a hand in front of her face.

Tink blinked. Thinking about oven timers had given her an idea. "I think I know how to fix you," she told Trindle.

"Wonderful!" Trindle exclaimed. She glanced at the tools on Tink's worktable and gulped. "Er . . . will it hurt much?"

Tink didn't hear her. She was busy collecting things from around her work-shop—a scrap of wood, a nail, a sliver of metal, some pots of paint.

She brought everything over to the table. Trindle watched nervously as Tink picked up her hammer. For the next several minutes, the room was quiet as Tink tapped and tinkered.

At last she stepped back. "There it is, Trindle! The answer to your problem!"

Trindle stared at the object on the table. It was a wooden box with a little spinner in the center. The sections of the dial were painted different colors.

"What is it?" Trindle asked.

"It's a Decider," Tink replied. "When-

ever you can't decide what to wear, just spin the needle, like this." She flicked the spinner so it whirled on its pin. "Whatever color it lands on, that's what you should wear."

"Let me try." Trindle reached for the

Decider. "What should I wear today?" she asked aloud. She flicked the spinner. It spun round and round and came to a stop on blue.

Trindle gasped. "It works! And I know just the dress to wear—bluebells with a matching blue bonnet! Oh, Tink, how can I ever thank you?"

Tink waved a hand. "It's no trouble at all."

"I know! I'll make you a dress!" Trindle exclaimed. "It will be—" She spun the dial. "A green dress! Would you like that?"

"That would be very nice," said Tink, ushering her to the door.

As Trindle flew away, Tink could hear her saying, "What color should I wear tomorrow? . . . Ooh, red! And what color should I wear the day after that? . . . Ooh, purple! . . ."

"Finally, some peace and quiet," Tink said to herself. "Now I can get around to fixing Lily's rake."

4

But no sooner had Tink picked up her hammer than the bell over her door jingled again.

Tink looked up with a sigh. "Now what?"

A round sparrow man with rosy cheeks flew in. His name was Rolo, and he was a messenger talent. "Tink!" he burst out.

"Thank goodness you're here."

The tips of Tink's wings quivered. "Do you have a message for me?"

"No, no," said Rolo. "I need your help." He leaned closer and lowered his voice. "Can you keep a secret?"

Tink nodded.

"Well, I can't!" Rolo burst out. "No matter how hard I try. Whenever I hear an interesting tidbit, I can't keep it to myself. I just have to tell someone!"

Tink smiled. She already knew this about Rolo—everyone in Pixie Hollow did. There was no faster way to spread a bit of news than to ask Rolo not to tell anyone.

"What's so bad about that?" she asked.

"I'm a messenger," Rolo explained. "Fairies trust me to carry their news safely. But how can they when I always spill it? That's why I'm here, Tink. I need you to fix me."

"But I don't fix fairies," Tink explained. "I only fix pots and pans and things."

"You fixed Dooley," Rolo pointed out. "He says you're the best fix-it fairy around."

The best fix-it fairy around. The words rang in Tink's ears. It was the exact same thing Trindle had said. Tink liked the sound of it.

"Maybe I can help," she told him.

Tink reached into a little drawer in her worktable. She pulled out a small

magnifying glass. She began to examine Rolo, just as she would a pot or a pan.

She peeked into Rolo's ears. She looked into his eyes. "Open wide," she said as she peered into his mouth.

"What are you looking for?" Rolo asked.

"Leaks," said Tink.

Finding no leaks, Tink put the magnifying glass away. She tugged her bangs, thinking. If leaks weren't the problem, then what was?

Maybe Rolo is like a pot that keeps boiling over, Tink decided. *Every time he has a secret, he bubbles up and spills it.* Tink only knew one way to fix such a pot—put a lid on it!

She went over to the corner of her

workshop and began to rummage around. At last, under a pile of polishing rags, she found what she was looking for. It was a metal box with a little silver key. She brought them to Rolo.

"This is a Secret Keeper," she told him. "Carry it with you at all times. Whenever you have a secret, whisper it into the box and then lock it. Your secret will be safe."

Rolo turned the box around in his hands. "How does it work?"

"I can't tell you," Tink said, giving him a mysterious smile.

Rolo winked. "Oh, I get it! You have a Secret Keeper, too! What a clever invention. You're brilliant, Tink!" And tucking the box under his arm, he flew out the door.

Tink sighed with satisfaction. How she loved a job well done!

She sat back down at her worktable and picked up Lily's rake. But she just couldn't concentrate. She was still thinking about Trindle and Rolo. Tink had never realized how much fun fixing a fairy could be. It was as good as fixing pots and pans.

In fact, it's even better than fixing pots and pans, Tink thought. What pot had ever said, "You're brilliant, Tink"? What pan had exclaimed, "How can I ever thank you?"

Was this what Spring had meant by "bigger things"? Tink wondered. Were there other fairies out there who needed her help?

That moment, the door of the workshop burst open yet again. Tink's friend Rosetta, a garden-talent fairy, flew in.

"Tinker Bell!" she cried. "I need your help!"

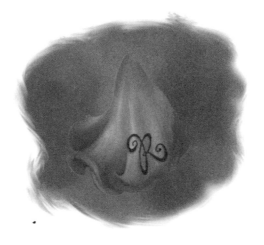

5

"WHAT'S WRONG, ROSETTA?" Tink asked in alarm.

The garden fairy's face was pale. Her wings trembled. Tink realized she was quite upset.

Rosetta flung herself onto a stool next to Tink's workbench. She put her wrist to her forehead and fluttered her long eyelashes. "Oh, Tink," she wailed. "It's a disaster!"

"What is it?" asked Tink. "A broken fence post? A hole in a bucket?"

Rosetta shook her head. "Worse than that."

Tink tried to think what was worse than a hole in a bucket. "A wheelbarrow without a wheel?"

"No." Rosetta sighed. "It's Herk."

"Herk?" Tink asked. "You mean the harvest talent? What did *he* do?"

"He hasn't done a thing," Rosetta sniffled. "That's just it. I might as well be a gnat, for all he notices me." She blew her nose into a rose-petal hanky. "You don't think I'm a gnat, do you, Tink?"

Tink scratched her head. What was

Rosetta talking about? She couldn't make any sense of it. "You're nothing like a gnat," she told her friend. "You're much nicer and prettier. And better dressed."

"Do you think so?" For a moment, Rosetta looked pleased. She smoothed her dress. It was made of pink rose petals, with red buttons.

But a moment later, Rosetta's face crumpled. "Oh, what does it matter if I have a pretty dress when I don't have anyone to dance with!" she wailed.

Tink patted her hand. But she was more confused than ever. First gnats, and now dances? What was going on?

"All alone . . . ," Rosetta said between sobs. "Dance . . . and he couldn't care less. . . . Tink, my heart is *broken*!"

"Your *heart?*" Tink asked. Her eyes widened.

Rosetta nodded. "That's why I'm here." She dabbed at her eyes. "I was hoping you could help me. They say you're the best fix-it fairy around."

Rosetta wants me to fix her broken heart! Tink thought. She had never fixed anything like that before. She wondered how it was done. It couldn't be easy.

But I'll have to try, she decided bravely. Rosetta was her friend, and she clearly needed Tink's help.

Rosetta looked up at her through wet eyelashes. "Tink, I feel awful. It's as if there's an empty space right here." She tapped the place over her heart.

"Oh, dear." Tink clutched her head. Could she patch up a broken heart with some putty? Or maybe a bit of wood? Or Never silver?

"Will you help me?" Rosetta asked.

"I'll do everything I can," Tink promised her friend.

As if a cloud had lifted, Rosetta's face suddenly brightened. "I knew I could count on you!"

"It's the least I can do," Tink said. But she was worried that this might be her most difficult job yet.

First things first, she decided. Before she could fix the cracked heart, she needed to know how big the problem was. She put her ear close to Rosetta's back.

Rosetta frowned. "What in the name of Never Land are you doing?"

"Shhh!" Tink put a finger to her lips. "I'm listening for the crack."

Rosetta stepped back. "The crack? Tink, what are you talking about? I thought you said you'd help me."

"I'm trying to," Tink told her. "But

I have to know how big the hole is before I can fix you."

"Fix *me?*" Rosetta exclaimed. "What about *Herk?*"

"What about him?" asked Tink, startled.

Rosetta sighed and put her hands on her hips. "Tink, haven't you been listening to a word I've said?"

Finally, Rosetta explained. The full-moon dance was coming up soon, and Rosetta had her heart set on dancing with Herk. But Herk didn't want to go to the dance.

"I've done everything I can think of," Rosetta told Tink. "I wore my nicest dress. I smiled my friendliest smile. I even showed off my dancing skills with

a few twirls in the tearoom. But he still doesn't notice me."

Sadly, Rosetta lowered her eyes and pursed her lips. "I need you to fix Herk. Make him go to the full-moon dance with me," she said.

"How can I make him go to the dance if he doesn't want to?" Tink asked.

"You're the best fix-it fairy in Pixie Hollow. You'll find a way. And besides, you promised you'd help me," Rosetta reminded her.

Tink sighed. "I did, didn't I?"

"You can find Herk in the orchard," Rosetta told her. "Now I'm off to watch the fast-flying races. Don't forget to let me know what he says!"

She wiggled her fingers at Tink and

flew to the door. Then she darted back. "And don't tell him I sent you!" She flew away.

Tink stared after her. She had no idea what to do next.

But a promise was a promise. Tink squared her shoulders and set out for the orchard to see if she could fix Herk.

6

IN THE ORCHARD, harvest talents wove in and out of the trees' branches, plucking fruit for the kitchen. It was hard, dangerous work. They wore walnut-shell helmets to protect their heads from falling fruit.

Tink flew over to a little group of fairies. They were piling cherries near the roots of a tree.

"I'm looking for Herk," Tink said. "Can you tell me where he is?"

One of the fairies pushed back her helmet and squinted. "Try that crab apple tree," she said. She pointed to a tree that was heavy with fruit.

Tink thanked the fairy and started toward the tree.

"Wait!" said the fairy, calling her back. She took off her helmet and handed it to Tink. "You'll need this."

Tink put on the helmet and flew over to the crab apple tree. She spotted Herk among the leaves. Herk was one of the largest sparrow men in Pixie Hollow. He had a broad, square head and wings as big as a meadowlark's. Tink noticed he wasn't wearing a helmet.

"Herk!" she called to get his attention.

Herk didn't seem to hear her. He had both arms wrapped around a crab apple. He was trying to wrestle it from the branch.

Tink flew closer. "Herk!" she said again.

"*Grrrr!*" Herk grunted. He strained with all his might. The crab apple still clung to the branch.

As Herk pulled, he shook the tree branch, causing other fruit to fall.

Tink ducked as crab apples rained down around them. Soon there was a pile of fruit on the ground.

But Herk didn't seem to notice. With one last tug, he finally managed to pluck the crab apple.

"Got one!" he bellowed, holding it

up. Just then, he noticed Tink. "Tinker Bell, what are you doing here?"

Tink landed on the branch next to him. She glanced down at the fruit on the ground. "Shouldn't you be wearing a helmet, Herk?" she asked.

"Nah! Not me! My head's hard as a rock," he replied proudly. He rapped it with his knuckles to prove it.

At that moment, one last crab apple fell. It whistled down and bonked Herk right on the head.

Tink gasped. "Are you all right?"

"What did I tell you? Hard as a rock," said Herk, looking at Tink cross-eyed.

Tink decided she had better get on with fixing Herk. "You know, there's a full-moon festival coming up soon. Have you thought about who you'll dance with yet?" she asked.

"I don't like to dance," said Herk.

"That's silly," said Tink. "Everyone likes to dance!"

"Not me," said Herk.

"When was the last time you tried?" Tink challenged him.

"Well." He glanced right and left, then lowered his voice. "The thing is, I don't know how to dance."

Is that all? thought Tink. Fixing Herk would be a breeze! All she had to do was teach him.

"It's easy," she said. "I'll show you how."

"Here?" Herk looked around. "Now?"

"Why not?" said Tink. "No one can

see us. The leaves of the tree will keep us hidden. Now, watch me."

Tink fluttered up in the air. She opened her arms wide and did a little twirl. "Now you try it," she told him.

Herk fluttered up next to her. He opened his arms wide—and smacked Tink.

"Whoops," said Herk.

"It's okay." Tink checked her arm for a bruise. "Twirls are hard. Maybe we should try something easier. Like a swoop! Watch this."

Tink dove off the branch and swooped through the air. She ended with a flourish. "Your turn," she told Herk.

Herk took a deep breath and dove off the branch. But when he tried the flourish, his wings got tangled. He crashed into Tink. They both slammed into a branch.

"Are you all right?" Herk asked as he helped her up.

Tink rubbed her sore knee. Fixing Herk was turning out to be more dangerous than she'd imagined.

But I promised Rosetta, Tink reminded herself. *I can't give up yet.*

"Swoops are tricky," Tink told Herk. "Anyway, all you really need to know for the full-moon dance is the spin. We can do that together!"

Tink held on to both of Herk's hands. Flapping their wings, they began to spin around.

"See?" said Tink. "It's easy!"

"Look, I'm dancing!" Herk whooped with delight.

Round and round they went. They whipped through the air, faster and faster . . . too fast!

"Slow down!" Tink cried. They were spinning out of control!

"*Ahhh!*" Tink yelled as they crashed

through the tree's leaves. They bounced off a branch. Crab apples started to fall again.

Tink and Herk stopped spinning. They ducked for cover as the hard crab apples dropped all around them.

Just when they thought it was safe, one last crab apple fell. It bopped Tink on top of her walnut-shell helmet. "*Ow!*" she squealed.

Herk shook his head. "Maybe we should just forget the lesson. I'll never learn to dance," he said.

"But you have to!" Tink cried in exasperation. "There's a very special fairy who wants to dance with you!"

"There is?" Herk asked.

Tink nodded. "She told me herself."

"She did?" A smile spread across Herk's broad face. "Who is it?"

"I'll give you a hint," said Tink. "She's pretty as a *flower*."

Herk's face brightened. "Is it Sparkle?"

"No," said Tink with a little frown. "What I meant to say is, she's pretty as a *rose*."

"Hmmm," said Herk. "Is it Spring? Silvermist?"

Tink tugged her bangs. She was starting to think that Herk had been hit on the head by one too many crab apples. "I'll give you one last hint. This certain fairy has been paying a lot of special attention to you!"

"Special attentio— Oh!" Herk's eyes widened. He stared at Tink.

Tink grinned. At last she had gotten through! "So, do you think you might like to be her dancing partner, too?" she asked slyly.

Herk's glow turned orange as he blushed. "I—I guess so," he stammered.

"Well, then!" said Tink. "We'd better teach you how to dance!"

One hour—and many more bruises—later, Tink had finally managed to teach Herk the first few steps of the fairy pinwheel.

"Now promise me you'll practice," Tink said when their lesson was over.

Herk blushed orange again. Then he thanked Tink for her help.

As Tink flew back toward the Home Tree, she congratulated herself. *How glad Rosetta will be when she sees that Herk is fixed. Another job well done!*

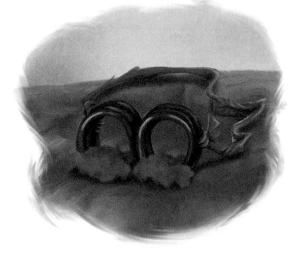

7

TINK WHISTLED HAPPILY as she landed in the Home Tree courtyard.

She looked around and sighed with contentment. "What a perfect day!" she said.

Tink spotted her friend Fawn, an animal-talent fairy. Fawn was on her way somewhere. *Probably going to visit her critter friends*, Tink thought. Fawn loved to play with the woodland creatures.

As Fawn zoomed past, Tink caught a whiff of badger.

"Phew!" said Tink, pinching her nose. "Fawn should do something about that smell!"

Across the courtyard was Bess. Tink waved to her art-talent friend. Bess had orange paint on her clothes, green paint in her hair, and a big blob of blue paint on the tip of her nose.

"What a mess!" Tink said to herself. Everywhere she looked, she saw fairies in need of fixing.

"Fly with you, Tink!" said a voice next to her.

Tink turned and saw her friend Rani.

She was sitting on a toadstool in the courtyard. Rani was a water-talent fairy. She had long, rippling hair and ocean-blue eyes, which at the moment were full of tears.

"Rani, what's wrong?" Tink asked.

"I'm just happy to see you!" Rani gave Tink a quick hug, and her tears spilled onto Tink's shoulder. As a water-talent fairy, Rani cried easily.

A bit too easily, Tink thought with a little frown. Rani was one of the kindest fairies she knew. But she was so weepy! *If only I could fix her.* And suddenly Tink thought of a way.

"Why are you looking at me like that?" Rani asked.

"Rani, come to my workshop in one

hour!" Tink said excitedly. "And bring Fawn and Bess, too. I'll have something exciting for all of you."

"Why?" asked Rani. "What is it?"

"You'll see," Tink said. "I'm going to fix everything!"

Tink darted back to her workshop and set to work. By the time Rani, Fawn, and Bess arrived, she had everything ready.

"Come in! Come in!" Tink beckoned her friends inside. "You'll be happy to know I've solved all your problems!"

"What problems?" asked Bess.

Tink didn't hear her. "Rani, these are for you," she said. She plucked a pair of goggles off her worktable and handed them to her friend. "Put them on."

Rani slipped the goggles over her head. The frames were made of copper wire. They had little bits of sea sponge attached to the bottom.

"How do I look?" Rani asked.

Fawn snorted. "Silly."

"They might not be pretty," Tink admitted. "But they serve a very useful purpose."

"What purpose?" asked Bess.

"They soak up tears!" Tink exclaimed. "Whenever you feel like crying, Rani, just put these goggles on, and *ta-da!* No more tears!"

Rani's forehead wrinkled. "You don't like tears?"

"Well, they are rather wet," replied Tink.

Rani blinked, and a few teardrops fell onto the sponges. Her feelings were hurt. But Tink was too caught up in her invention to notice.

"You see? They work!" she exclaimed.

"Yes, they do," Rani sniffled, and she hurried out the door.

"Don't forget—let them dry out between cries!" Tink called after her. She turned to find Fawn and Bess frowning at her. "What?"

"I *like* Rani's tears," said Fawn.

"They're part of what makes her Rani," Bess agreed.

Tink waved a hand. "She's still the same old Rani—just a little less damp! Now, for you, Fawn, I have something special. I know how much you love spending time with animals."

Fawn grinned. "And they love spending time with me."

Tink nodded. "Which is why I came up with this." She picked up a belt. A small glass bottle was attached to it. Tink fastened it around Fawn's waist.

"After every visit with a badger or a skunk, you just push this button." Tink pressed a little button on the belt. A misty cloud of sweet perfume sprayed out from the bottle. It settled over Fawn.

"*Yech!*" Fawn tried to wave the perfume away. "Why did you do that?"

"To fix the animal smell, of course," Tink explained. "Hold still, Fawn, or it won't work." She pressed the button again. More mist shot out.

"Stop! Stop!" Fawn shrieked.

"Now she smells like honeysuckle and badger," Bess noted, holding her nose.

"One more spritz should do it," Tink said. She tried to push the button again,

but Fawn ducked away. Tink chased her around the room.

"Tink, stop! Animals *hate* perfume!" Fawn cried. Dodging Tink's outstretched hands, she fled.

"Oh, well. Some fairies just don't know what's good for them." Tink sighed and turned to her remaining friend. "And now, for you, Bess—Bess?" Tink looked around. "Where did she go?"

The room was empty. Bess, seeing her chance, had sneaked out the door while Tink wasn't looking.

"Well, I can fix Bess later," Tink said. "But what should I fix now?"

Then she heard a voice outside—a terrible, shrill voice. "I would *never* carry a daisy-petal parasol. They *wilt*, you know.

Magnolia petals are much sturdier."

That voice! Tink shuddered. She looked out the door and saw Iris talking to two other fairies. Or rather, Tink saw Iris talking—and two other fairies flying quickly away.

If there was ever a fairy who needed fixing, it's Iris, Tink thought. Iris was bossy. She was irritating. And her voice was worse than Dooley's squeaky wheel. It was a voice that needed fixing.

Not that fixing Iris will be easy, Tink thought. A slow grin spread across her face. Lucky for Iris, she was up to the challenge!

8

BY THE NEXT MORNING, Tink had figured out a way to fix Iris. Bright and early, she went to Lily's garden. Tink was dragging a big, lumpy sack with her.

Lily was already working in the garden. She was digging holes for carrot seeds. When she saw Tink, Lily put down her shovel and dusted off her hands. "Tink,

I didn't think I'd see you so soon," she said. "Have you fixed my rake already?"

The rake! Tink had been so busy fixing fairies, she'd forgotten all about it. "No, not yet," she admitted. "I'll fix it soon."

Lily peered curiously at the sack. "What have you got there?" she asked.

"It's for Iris," Tink replied. "Have you seen her?"

"Iris?" Lily nodded. "She's over—"

"*Unbelievable!*" interrupted a shrill voice. It was coming from a corner of the garden. Tink turned and saw Iris hovering next to a cluster of daisies.

"These flowers' stems are *bent!*" Iris declared, to no one in particular. "When I had a garden, my daisies were *straight as fence posts!*"

"Never mind," Tink told Lily. "I see her."

Tink flew over to Iris and set down her sack. "Iris! You're just the fairy I've been looking for."

"I suppose you're here for my lecture on dandelions," said Iris.

Tink shook her head. "I didn't know about it."

"I put up posters in the tearoom." Iris glanced around, looking for the rest of the audience. "I thought more fairies would have come by now."

"Well, why don't you start? Maybe more fairies will turn up soon," Tink suggested. A lecture was the perfect chance for her to fix Iris's voice!

Iris picked up her big plant book and

turned to a page. In a voice like rusty nails, she began to read, "'The *fierce dandelion* is the king of flowers—'"

"Wait!" Tink cried, holding up her hands.

Iris looked up. "What's wrong?"

"Before you go on, you need this." Tink untied the top of the sack. It fell away, revealing a shiny silver contraption. It looked a bit like a tuba, but bigger. It had a long neck that wound around and around in twists and turns and spirals. The end of the instrument flared out like a big silver flower.

"What is it?" Iris asked.

"It's a Voice Fixer-Upper," Tink said.

"What does it do?"

"You just talk into this end." Tink

pointed to the narrow end of the instrument. "Then your voice travels through
all these twists and turns and comes out
here." She pointed to the flowerlike open-
ing. "And it sounds better than ever."

Tink had stayed up all night hammer-

ing the thing together from tubes and pipes and scraps of metal. She thought it was her finest invention yet.

"Go ahead," she told Iris. "Try it."

Iris put her mouth close to the narrow end. She cleared her throat. "As I was saying, 'The fierce dandelion is the king of flowers . . .'"

As Iris spoke into the machine, a beautiful voice came out the other end. It was as clear as crystal and as soft as a summer breeze. Even the birds in the trees stopped singing to listen.

"It works!" Tink clapped her hands together with glee.

"'Do not mistake the dandelion for a simple weed.'" Iris went on with her lecture. "'It is, in fact, a cunning predator.'" Each word rang like the chime of a silver bell.

Lily came flying over. "What's that lovely sound?" she asked Tink.

Tink pointed proudly to Iris and the Voice Fixer-Upper. She felt tears in her eyes. She'd done it! She'd fixed Iris! Oh, it was glorious!

Other fairies and sparrow men had started to poke their heads into Lily's garden to see where the sound was coming from.

"Ah!" said Iris. "More fairies have come to hear my lecture." She began to speak a little more loudly.

The problem was that Iris couldn't hear herself. The end of the Voice Fixer-Upper was pointed away from her. To

Iris's own ears, she sounded the same as always.

"I can't hear anything. Is this thing even working?" she asked Tink, fiddling with the Voice Fixer-Upper.

"Be careful!" cried Tink.

But Iris wasn't listening. Before Tink could stop her, Iris had wrenched the wide flower end right off the machine. She held it up to her lips like a megaphone.

"Can every fairy hear me?" she screeched.

Now, imagine the scream of a hawk, the squeak of a rusty hinge, and the squeal of chalk on a chalkboard all rolled together. Iris's shout was ten times worse. All the fairies' hair stood on end.

"I say!" Iris remarked. "That's much better!"

Using the end of the Voice Fixer-Upper like a megaphone, Iris continued her lecture.

"Stop! Stop!" Tink cried. It was unbearable.

Iris scowled at her. "Didn't anyone ever teach you not to interrupt?" she snapped. Then Iris carried on, her voice booming across the garden. Around her, flowers wilted. Fairies cowered. Birds flew away.

Still Iris talked on.

Tink was near tears. This wasn't how things were supposed to go at all!

"What should I do?" she yelled to Lily.

Lily's hands were firmly clamped over her ears. But she could read Tink's lips. She shrugged.

"Cover your ears," she said. "And hope it's a short lecture!"

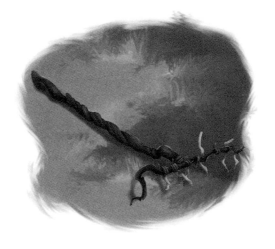

9

TINK WAS NOT one to give up easily. Despite the Voice Fixer-Upper disaster, she was still determined to fix Iris's voice.

She tried everything she could think of. She wrapped a spider-silk scarf around Iris's neck, hoping the warmth would help. But Iris complained loudly about the color. Tink encouraged her to whisper. But that only made Iris talk more loudly. Tink even made her gargle with honeysuckle nectar. But it turned out Iris liked to sing when she gargled.

"... *glurg-glurg—fly with me, fairy—glurg* ... ," Iris gargle-sang.

Iris's singing voice was even worse than her regular voice.

"Well, that was nice," Iris said when she was done gargling. Her voice hadn't improved one bit. "But I think now I could use a little tea. Tink, why don't you get me some?"

Tink scowled and flew over to Lily. "Iris acts like I'm her helper!" she complained.

"You have been paying her a lot of attention," Lily pointed out.

"I'm just trying to fix her voice. But I don't know what to do next," Tink said.

Lily picked up her watering can and sprinkled water over a cluster of posies. "Maybe the reason you can't fix Iris's voice," she replied, "is because she doesn't want it fixed."

"How could she not want it fixed?" asked Tink. "It's awful!"

"Maybe it's just what makes her unique," Lily said.

But Tink wasn't listening anymore. Something had caught her eye. Not far away, in the Home Tree courtyard, she saw Rosetta practicing the pinwheel dance. Rosetta's arm was linked through a sparrow man's. They spun in a circle, each using one wing to fly.

Look how well Herk dances, Tink thought with a smile. *Look how happy Rosetta seems.* At least *that* fix-it job had gone right.

But just then the couple spun around. Tink caught a glimpse of the sparrow man's face. It wasn't Herk after all. It was a fast flier named Blaze!

"Rosetta!" Tink yelled. "What are you doing?"

Rosetta smiled and flew over. Her cheeks were rosy and her eyes were bright. "Tink, isn't it wonderful?" she said. "Blaze is going to be my dancing partner in the full-moon dance!"

"But—but—but—" Tink stuttered. "But I thought you wanted *Herk* to be your dancing partner."

"That was before I ran into Blaze at the fast-flying races," Rosetta explained. "You know, you were right. The problem wasn't Herk, it was me—but now everything has worked out for the best."

This was terrible! Herk was going to be so upset. "Why didn't you *tell* me?" Tink asked Rosetta.

Rosetta looked surprised. "I thought everyone in Pixie Hollow knew! I told

Rolo yesterday—and you know *he* can't keep a secret."

Tink's mind reeled. Oh, this was bad! She'd fixed Rolo *too* well!

"Now my only problem is what to wear," Rosetta babbled on. "I asked Trindle to make my dress. She usually has the most exciting outfits. But lately her clothes have been so . . . well, *boring*. Look, you can see for yourself. Here she comes now."

Rosetta pointed to Trindle, who was flying toward them. The sewing fairy was dressed head to toe in yellow buttercups.

Rosetta shook her head. "You see what I mean, Tink? She's all dressed in one color. Everyone's saying she's lost her touch."

Tink clutched her head. It was too much. She'd fixed Trindle—and now she was going to have to *un*-fix her!

But, Tink decided, *first I'd better find Herk.* She needed to explain what had happened before she had *another* broken heart to fix.

Tink turned to leave—and came face to face with Herk himself.

"There you are, Tink!" he exclaimed. "I've been looking all over for you!"

Tink gulped. Had Herk seen Rosetta dancing with Blaze? Was he angry now? Were his feelings hurt? "I can explain—" she began.

"I don't need you to explain," Herk interrupted. "I just need practice! I've got to get all the steps right if I'm going to be your partner at the full-moon dance."

"My partner!" Tink exclaimed.

"That's what you wanted, isn't it?" he said, suddenly looking uncertain.

Oh, no. Just thinking about dancing with Herk made Tink feel black and blue and sore all over. Somehow her fix-it job had gone terribly wrong. Now she had to choose between breaking Herk's heart— and risking her own neck!

Before Tink could answer, Trindle flew up. "Oh, Tink," she said. "I'm so glad I found you. I've got a big problem— pink!"

"Pink?" Tink echoed faintly.

Trindle held up the spinner Tink had made. "I've got red, orange, yellow, green, blue, and purple, but there's no pink.

How do I decide if I want to wear pink?"

Pink was the least of Tink's problems! Tink opened her mouth to reply. But as she did, she felt a tap on her shoulder. She turned and saw Rolo.

"Tink!" he whispered. "You've got to help me! I've lost the key!" He held up the little box Tink had given him. "All the secrets are still inside! What should I do?"

What should I do? Tink thought desperately. Everyone needed her help. And she didn't know how to help any of them! She looked from one face to the next.

"Tink?" said Rosetta.

"Tink?" said Herk.

"Tink?" said Trindle.

"Tink?" said Rolo.

"TINK!" Iris screeched. *"Where's my tea?"*

That voice! Tink couldn't stand it a moment longer. Without thinking, she snatched the watering can from Lily's hand and poured it over Iris's head.

Water dripped from Iris's hair. It slid from her nose. It pooled around her wings. Iris's mouth opened.

"EEEEEEEEEEEEEEEEE!"

Iris's shriek was so loud and so shrill that creatures as far away as the Mermaid Lagoon had to cover their ears. All over Pixie Hollow, mirrors shattered. Soufflés collapsed. Milk soured in the milking buckets.

When Iris was done, there was a stunned silence. Rosetta, Herk, Trindle,

and Rolo all turned to glare at Tink.

"What did you do that for?" Rosetta demanded.

"Yeah," agreed Herk. "She was only asking a question."

Tink looked around at their angry faces. At that moment, she realized that fairies were nothing like pots and pans. They never did what you expected. And they were very, very hard to fix.

Suddenly, Tink remembered Lily's rake back in her workshop—a nice, quiet rake, waiting patiently for her attention. At that moment, Tink wanted nothing more than to be working on it.

Without a word, Tink set down the bucket and flew away.

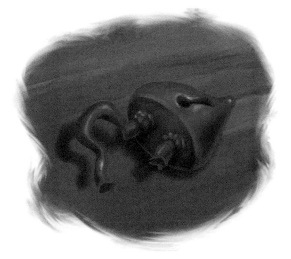

10

"THERE YOU ARE, Lily. Good as new," Tink said a few days later. "Well, almost, anyway."

Tink handed the repaired rake to her friend. She had straightened every one of the tines and fixed the broken piece. But she hadn't polished the handle. She guessed Lily might prefer it the way it was.

"It's perfect!" Lily gushed. "Oh, I'm so glad to have it back." She combed it across the grass a few times, just to try it out. "Thank you, Tink. I'd like to do something nice for you, too. Can you stay for tea?"

Tink shook her head. "Another time. I have something important to finish right now."

As Tink flew back to her workshop, she spotted Rolo in front of the Home Tree. He was whispering something in a fairy's ear.

Tink smiled to herself. The day before, Rolo had brought the Secret Keeper into her workshop, and together they'd broken the lock. Tink had promised to fix it. But she had a feeling that it was one

repair she'd never get around to making. Rolo didn't seem to miss it.

And there, passing through the courtyard, was Trindle. Tink waved to her, and Trindle waved back. She was dressed in a full-length orange tiger lily dress, with green spider-silk stockings and a red mushroom cap. The Decider was still in Tink's workshop, too, waiting for her to add pink.

"I'll get around to fixing that Decider one of these days," Tink called out to Trindle.

"Take your time!" Trindle called back.

Tink grinned. She'd known Trindle wouldn't need the Decider anytime soon. Rosetta had praised Trindle's wild outfits so much that Tink had a feeling

Trindle would never go back to wearing just one color.

As for Rosetta, Tink hadn't seen her in days. She was too busy practicing with her two dancing partners—Blaze *and* Herk.

Tink arrived at her workshop. She went inside and sat down at the table. But she'd only just begun tap-tapping with her tinker's hammer when the bell over the door jingled. Dooley came in.

"Fly with you," Tink said to him. "What's new today?"

"Nothing good," Dooley replied with a woeful sigh. "My ear itches, and I've got a hole in my sock. I took a wrong turn getting here. And this morning at breakfast my tea was cold. Ah, me.

It's a sad, sad life for poor old Dooley."

Tink shook her head. "I wish I could help you," she told him. "But I don't fix fairies."

"Oh, that's not why I'm here, Tink. I came about my wheel." Dooley set a rusted old wagon wheel on the table. "The wheel's got a wobble, you see. Not that anything can be done about it," he added glumly.

But Tink brightened. "A wobbly wheel? Why didn't you say so! I'll have it fixed in no time. Just put it on the workbench there."

Dooley did as she said, then turned to leave. But something on Tink's worktable caught his eye. "Say, that's nice! What is it?"

Tink held up the necklace she was making. It had a silver pendant shaped like a flower with three curling petals.

"It's an iris for Iris," she explained. "I thought I ought to do something nice for her. She put up with a lot from me."

Dooley took the necklace and turned it over in his hands. "It's awful pretty. But there's a flaw here." He pointed to a rough spot on the edge of the iris.

"I know," said Tink. "I put it there."

"What for?" asked Dooley.

"It makes it more interesting," said Tink. "It's a bit like fairies themselves. After all, who doesn't have a flaw?"

Dooley raised his eyebrows thoughtfully. "I'd say you're right about that, Tink. Anyway, I'll bet Iris will like the necklace." He handed it back.

Dooley bid Tink good-bye. Then he left the workshop, singing to himself.

"I've got a hole in my sock
And a cold cup of tea.

There's an itch in my ear—
Ah, woe is me. . . ."

Tink smiled and shook her head. "Funny old Dooley," she said.

Then, with a happy sigh, she got back to work.

Don't miss any of the magical
Disney Fairies chapter books!

Queen Clarion's Secret

Just as Prilla was about to land, a shadow crossed the ground in front of her. She looked up and her eyes widened. A huge bird was soaring across the sky. It was unlike any bird Prilla had ever seen. The bird was as colorful as a parrot, but it was much longer. Its wingspan was as wide as an eagle's.

The bird traveled so fast that it left a multi-colored streak in the sky behind it. Prilla felt a shiver of fear. A bird so big and fast could be dangerous to fairies. She would have to warn the queen.

But when she looked back, Queen Clarion was gone.

Myka Finds Her Way

Myka had to get closer. She had to see what was happening. She flew toward the noise and lights. The rumblings turned to roars. The flashes grew brighter.

Everything looked strange in the on-again, off-again flare of light. *Boom!*

She saw a gnarled tree bent over, its bare branches sweeping the ground. *Boom!* She spotted a towering beehive. It swayed from the thick trunk of a maple tree.

She swerved around it and kept flying. *Boom!* The spooky light cast long shadows from trees . . . plants . . . rocks. Everything seemed different. But she was a scout. She had to keep going.

Vidia Meets Her Match

Wisp's whole face lit up. "Race? With you? I'd love to!" she cried. "I hear you're the fastest fairy in Pixie Hollow."

"Mmm. Well, we'll see, won't we?" said Vidia.

Wisp's wings were already humming. "Where should we race?" she asked.

Vidia looked around. "From here to that tree," she decided. She pointed to a peach tree at the edge of the orchard. "To finish, touch the peach hanging from that low branch. Ready?"

Wisp nodded. The two got on their marks.

"Set . . . ," said Vidia.

They spread their wings.

"Go!"

Silvermist and
the Ladybug Curse

By now, other fairies had gathered around Silvermist. The ladybug sat perfectly still atop the water-talent fairy's head.

"You know," a garden-talent fairy named Rosetta mused, "there's an old superstition about white ladybugs. They're supposed to bring—"

"Bad luck!" Iris said, screeching to a stop in front of Silvermist.

A few fairies chuckled uncertainly. No one took Iris very seriously. But fairies were superstitious creatures. They believed in wishes, charms, and luck—both good and bad.

"The white ladybug!" Iris's voice rose higher and higher. "It's cursed!"

Prilla and the Butterfly Lie

An uncomfortable silence filled the tearoom. Some fairies studied their forks. Others examined their dinner plates very closely. No one would look up.

"No volunteers," said the queen. "This is indeed a problem. What are we to do?"

"I know!" said a voice. "There is a fairy who would be happy to help out. She *loves* butterflies."

The room began to buzz once more. Everyone wondered who the butterfly-loving fairy could be.

Prilla sank into her chair until her head was barely level with the table. She had completely forgotten about her butterfly lie.

Tink, North of Never Land

She'd been flying for a quarter of an hour when she looked down. Her heart sank. She was just crossing Havendish Stream.

At this rate, it will take me weeks to reach the Northern Shore! she thought.

But as luck would have it, the wind suddenly shifted in Tink's direction. She felt the carrier bumping against her heels.

Tink climbed into the basket. She let the wind speed her along. In no time, she had reached the edge of Pixie Hollow. Never Land's forest spread out below her like a great dark sea.